"Hey! I wonder what Handy is building over there," Chuck says. "I'm gonna check it out!"

3

"Hey there, Chuck," Handy says as Chuck rolls up.
"Check out this cool new obstacle course I'm building -
just like the ones in the Great Truck Games!"

"It has ramps and bridges and everything!" Handy announces excitedly.

"Wow! It's so cool!" says Chuck in awe.

Then, Chuck gets an idea. "Hey, I know. Let's pretend we're competing in the Great Truck Games!"

As Chuck races off, Handy calls after him. "Chuck, wait! It's not finished yet!"

But it's too late. Chuck zooms up the hill, full speed ahead to the bridge.

"Gee, this looks kinda tricky," Chuck thinks as he starts to cross the bridge. "But Great Truck Games champions never give up!"

Handy watches nervously as Chuck tries to make his way across. "Be careful, Chuck!" Handy calls.

But Chuck can't hear Handy from way up at the top of the bridge. He continues to speed across until, suddenly, he hears something rumbling. "What was that?" Chuck says.

He looks across the bridge to see a huge boulder coming right at him! He spins his tires, trying to back up, but his back tire gets stuck in a hole in the bridge. "Handy! Help! I'm stuck!" Chuck yells.

"On my way, good buddy!" Handy yells as he
races to save Chuck.

Handy tosses his tow hook. "I'll cut the boulder off at the pass!" he shouts.

The tow hook tears out just enough of the bridge
planks to let the boulder splash into the water below.

"Now to catch Chuck!" Handy pulls at the bridge with all his might.

"Wheeee!" Chuck exclaims as he soars into the air. "Time for one of my super-duper, amazingly incredible backflips!"

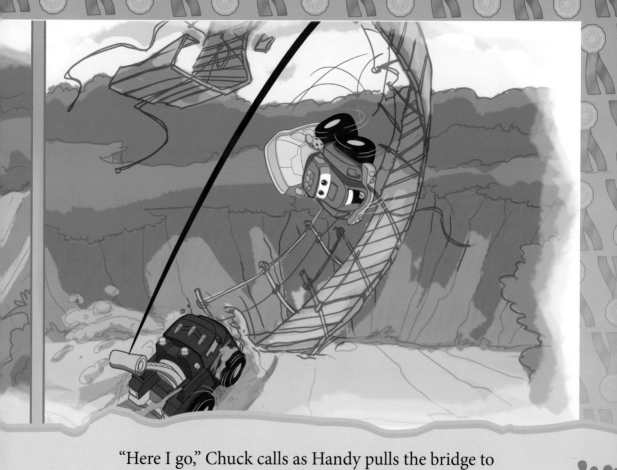

"Here I go," Chuck calls as Handy pulls the bridge to help Chuck get down. "Look out, Handy. I'm coming in for a landing!"

With Chuck back on solid ground, he speeds over to
Handy. "Great landing," he tells Handy. "But I think
YOU deserve the gold medal for getting me out of a
tough spot. You're a champion friend!"
"Cool, thanks!" exclaims Handy.

"Guess that leaves only one thing left to say," Chuck says.

"What's that?" Handy asks.

"Let's do it again!"